EHRENGARD

Isak Dinesen was the pen-name of Karen Blixen, who was born in Rungsted, Denmark, in 1885. After studying art at Copenhagen, Paris and Rome, she married her cousin, Baron Bror Blixen-Finecke, in 1914. Together they went to Kenya to manage a coffee plantation. After their divorce in 1921, she continued to run the plantation until a collapse in the coffee market forced her back to Denmark in 1931.

Although she had written occasional contributions to Danish periodicals since 1905 (under the *nom-de-plume* of Osceola), her real début took place in 1934 with the publication of *Seven Gothic Tales*, written in English under her pen-name. In 1937 she published, under her own name, *Out of Africa* (Penguin, 1954), an autobiographical account of the many years she spent in Kenya. Most of her subsequent books were published in English and Danish simultaneously, including *Winter's Tales* (1942, Penguin 1983) and *The Angelic Avengers* (1946), under the name of Pierre Andrézel. Among her other collections of stories are *Last Tales* (1957), *Anecdotes of Destiny* (1958), *Shadows on the Grass* (1960, Penguin 1984) and *Ehrengard* (1963).

Baroness Blixen died in Rungsted in 1962.

ISAK DINESEN

(KAREN BLIXEN)

Ehrengard

PENGUIN BOOKS

Penguin Books Ltd, Harmondsworth, Middlesex, England
Viking Penguin Inc., 40 West 23rd Street, New York, New York 10010, U.S.A.
Penguin Books Australia Ltd, Ringwood, Victoria, Australia
Penguin Books Canada Limited, 2801 John Street, Markham, Ontario, Canada L3R 1B4
Penguin Books (N.Z.) Ltd, 182–190 Wairau Road, Auckland 10, New Zealand

First published in the U.S.A. by Random House, Inc. 1963
First published in Great Britain by the University of Chicago Press 1975
Published in Penguin Books 1986

Copyright 1962 by The Curtis Publishing Co.
Copyright 1963 by Rungstedlundfonden

This edition is published with the permission of the Rungstedlund Foundation

Printed and bound in Great Britain by
Cox & Wyman Ltd, Reading

Ehrengard

An old lady told this story.

A hundred and twenty years ago, she began, my story told itself, at greater length of time than you or I can give to it, and with a throng of details and particulars which we can never hope to know. The men and women who then gradually built it up, and to whom it was a matter of life and death, are all long gone. They may be, by this time and before the throne of the Lamb, occasionally exchanging a smile and a remark: "O yes! And do you remember . . . ?" The roads and paths on which it moved are overgrown with grass, or are no more to be found.

The very country in which it began, developed and came to an end, may be said to have faded out of existence. For it was, in those good days, a fair, free and flourishing small principality of old Germany, and its sovereign was responsible to no one but God in Heaven. But later on, when times and men grew harder, it was silently and sadly swallowed up into the great new German Empire.

I am not going to give you the real name of this country, nor of the ladies and gentlemen within my tale. These latter would not have liked me to do so. To them a name was a sacred thing, and with both pride and humility each of them held his or her name to be the noblest and most important—and the lasting—part of his or her person and existence. Moreover, these names are all well known, most of them appear-

ing and reappearing in the history of their country. The family upon which my story turns was
indeed no mere family but a house, and its good
or bad luck, its honor and disgrace, were no or-
dinary family matters, but dynastic concerns.

So to begin with, my dearest, I shall inform
you that the stage of our little comedy or trag-
edy was the lovely country and the fine city of
Babenhausen, and that you will be devoting your
attention to a chronicle of the Grand Ducal
house of Fugger-Babenhausen. And as in the
course of my narrative new gentlemen and ladies
make their appearance in it, I shall endeavor to
find a new noble name for each of them.

The story may be said to fall into three
parts, the first of which—although I fear that it
may seem to you a bit lengthy—is in reality only
a kind of prelude to the second and third.

And so we begin.

❧

The Grand Duke and Grand Duchess of
Babenhausen for a long time were childless and

grieved over their lot. Particular circumstances made the misfortune more fatal. For the Grand Duke was the last of his line, and should he leave no son after him, the ducal crown would pass to a lateral branch of the dynasty, of doubtful legitimacy and principles. Great disturbance in the state might be the consequence.

It was therefore a great joy and relief to the loyal subjects of Babenhausen as well as to the Grand Ducal couple themselves when, after a waiting time of fifteen years, an heir was born. His cousins of the lateral branch bit their fingers and now, the sweet hope before them gone, took no trouble at all about their reputation, but openly surrounded themselves with the malcontents of the country.

Young Prince Lothar grew up graceful and wise. His proud parents appointed the best teachers in the nation for him, and took care to keep the wickedness and vulgarity of the world from him. For sixteen or seventeen years things were as happy as possible. Then a curious and unexpected anxiety began to stir in the heart of the Grand Duchess.

Very old families will sometimes feel upon them the shadow of annihilation. The plant loses contact with the soil, and while it may still put forth a single flower of exquisite loveliness, the root withers. The Grand Duchess came to wonder whether her son were not all too perfect for this world.

There was in Prince Lothar's ethereal and serene beauty a strain of aloofness which set him alone amongst the youths of his court and his generation. While he was devoted to the arts, and was himself a distinguished dilettante in music and painting and a skilled botanist and astronomer, the actual human world around him seemed incapable of captivating or holding him. He was never known of his own accord to touch any human being, he even shrank a little from the caresses of his mother. The time arrived when the Grand Duchess thought it her duty to form plans for his marriage, and she found that to this youth, whom any princess might be happy to call husband, the idea of marriage was as remote as the idea of death.

All women in their heart feel that through

the toils of pregnancy and the pangs of child-birth they have become entitled to an everlasting life in the flesh and on the earth. The Grand Duchess might claim this reward before other ladies of Babenhausen inasmuch as she had entered into matrimony with the sole idea of maintaining an ancient noble house, and loyally had given herself over to her mission. She had been brought to understand that, by law of nature, a more ardent initiative was required by her partner in the task, and earlier in life the fact had vexed and upset her, and had even cost her tears. By now she had become fully reconciled to it. She watched the angelic face and figure of her son and was seized by a cruel apprehension. Had her loyalty, her exertions and pain, served to postpone by one generation only the extinction of the dynasty of Fugger-Babenhausen?

Till this time the Grand Duchess had preferred for the ducal household ladies of a certain age and of homely appearance. Now she gradually appointed more attractive representatives of the sex to her staff. She gave a number of court balls and she encouraged her son to frequent the opera and the ballet. The Prince danced at the balls and came back from the theater delighted. He admired beauty in women as he admired it in flowers and was ever courteous to the ladies. But *la belle passion* as his young companions knew it, to him seemed to remain alien. His mother became impatient with her ladies and with the stars of the stage. What were they about, she indignantly asked herself, to be such bunglers in their *métier de femme?*

It so happened that at this time the Grand Duchess was having her portrait painted by that great artist the Geheimrat Wolfgang Cazotte.

Herr Cazotte at the age of forty-five had painted the portraits of most queens and princesses of Europe and was persona grata at a dozen courts. His fresh and pure nudes were bought at fancy prices by the galleries. At the same time he was on easy and friendly terms with street hawkers, circus performers and flower girls. He had velvety brown eyes, a red mouth and a remarkably sweet voice.

Although more than twice the age of Prince Lothar, Herr Cazotte for some time had been his closest friend and most constant companion. The young Prince felt a sincere admiration for the artist's extraordinary gifts, and the two had long talks together on elevated matters.

The Grand Duchess so far had not favored the friendship, for if Herr Cazotte was famous as a portraitist of fair ladies, he was no less celebrated and talked about as their conqueror and seducer, the irresistible Don Juan of his age.

My great-grandmother, Countess von Gassner, was Herr Cazotte's friend. A long time ago, when he had been a very poor young boy of Babenhausen and she a very great lady and a *bel esprit* of the city, she had discovered his genius, had seen to it that he got a painting master and leisure for his studies, and had even for a while adopted him into her own house. Herr Cazotte had a gift for gratitude, and she on her side remembered him as the very last of the row of pretty youths whom she had helped to a career the two were dear to one another's heart. Later when she had lost her great beauty, she had retired out of the world to her chateau in the country and had not wanted any of her old friends to see her again. For many years she and he had not met. But they had kept up a correspondence which pleased them both, him because it was in itself inspiring to him, her because in his letters he addressed her as a woman who might still be desired. Herr Cazotte was a very discreet person and could keep a secret with anyone, but he made an exception with my great-grandmother and felt free to pass on to her any knowledge of his and even the secrets of his friends, aware that none of it would ever get any further. Most of my knowledge with regard to the story of Ehrengard I owe to his letters to her.

She expostulated with him on his fickleness, and he answered her:

Dear, adored Lady,

You call an artist a seducer and are not aware that you are paying him the highest of compliments. The whole attitude of the artist towards the Universe is that of a seducer.

For what does seduction mean but the ability to make, with infinite trouble, pa-

tience and perseverance, the object upon which you concentrate your mind give forth, voluntarily and enraptured, its very core and essence? Aye, and to reach, in the process, a higher beauty than it could ever, under any other circumstances, have attained? I have seduced an old earthenware pot and two lemons into yielding their inmost being to me, to become mine and, at that same moment, to become phenomena of overwhelming loveliness and delight.

But most of all to be seduced is the privilege of woman, the which man may well envy her. Where would you be, my proud ladies, if you did not recognize the seducer in every man within waft of your petticoats? For however admirable she be, the woman who does not awaken in man the instinct of seducer is like the horse of the Chevalier de Kerguelen, which had all the good qualities in the world, but which was dead. And what poor unworthy creatures would we men be, did we not endeavor to draw forth, like the violinist with the bow upon the strings, the full abundance and virtue of the instrument within our hands?

But do not imagine, wise and sagacious Mama, that the seducer's art must in each individual engagement fetch him the same trophy. There are women who give out the fullness of their womanhood in a smile, a side glance or a waltz, and others who will be giving it in their tears. I may drink off a bottle of Rhine wine to its last drop, but I sip only one glass of a fine, and there be rare vintages from which I covet nothing but the bouquet. The honest and loyal seducer, when he has obtained the smile, the side glance, the waltz or the tears, will uncover his head to the lady, his heart filled with gratitude, and will be dreading only one thing: that he may ever meet her again.

It was a symptom of the Grand Duchess' altered politics that she did now view Herr Cazotte with a lenient eye, that during the sittings she lent a gracious ear to his converse, airily expressed her own opinions on life, and in the end hinted at her misgivings with regard to her son. The slightest of hints was sufficient, the painter read the Grand Ducal mind like a book, and like an aeolian harp responded to its inaudible sigh.

"Let me," he said, "endeavor to give words to my sentiments. It is true that, generally speaking, in a boy or a youth the qualities of inexperience and intactness, and of innocence itself, are looked upon as merely negative traits, that is, as the absence of knowledge or of zeal. But there are natures of such rare nobility that with them no quality nor condition will ever be negative. Incorporated in such a mind anything partakes in its soundness and purity. To the plastic unity of an exalted spirit no conflict exists, but nature and ideal are one. Idea and action, too, are one, inasmuch as the idea is an action and the action an idea. When Prince Lothar makes his choice he will do so in an instant and with the wholeness of his nature. Today he watches his young friends dissipating their hearts in petty cash, he does not judge them, but he knows that their ways are not his way."

The Grand Duchess was comforted by Herr Cazotte's speech, she listened to his advice, and together they thought out a project.

For some time the Grand Duke and Grand Duchess had been urging their son to pay a visit to such courts of Europe as had princesses of his own age, while on his side Prince Lothar had longed to make a tour to the great centers of art in the company of his learned friend. Obviously now the two purposes might be combined. Herr Cazotte, acting as both worldly and spiritual attaché to the youth, would imperceptibly lead his steps to the desired goal. Prince Lothar at once delightedly agreed to the arrangement and looked forward to his aesthetic pilgrimage. The Grand Duchess and Herr Cazotte also, with much zeal, looked round in every direction.

Herr Cazotte from the beginning had had his eyes on a particular court, that of Leuchtenstein. The principality of Leuchtenstein was about the size of the Grand Duchy of Babenhausen and its ruling house in age and purity of blood vied with the Grand Duke's own. The worthy Prince of Leuchtenstein had unfortunately lost his consort, but was fortunate in possessing five fair daughters. On a former visit to the court Herr Cazotte had painted the portraits of the young ladies and had all the time been feeling that for the task he needed the brush of Master Greuze. Since then the two eldest princesses had made pretty marriages, the third in age, Princess Ludmilla, by now was seventeen years old.

If the princely house of Leuchtenstein, Herr Cazotte reasoned, were running any risk of decline and annihilation, it was not from withering or from losing contact with this world. The noble family might, on the very contrary, perish from mere exuberance of life, like a tree through a long time blooming and blossoming to excess. Within the cluster of Leuchtenstein maidens the artist had scented a quality of unconscious seductiveness, that rose-like fullness and fragrance which guilelessly allured the passer-by to pick the flower. He led his steps, and those of Prince Lothar, to Leuchtenstein.

Many tales in the course of time have come to surround Prince Lothar's courtship.

It was said that the youth, inspired by Herr Cazotte's description of Princess Ludmilla, had insisted on making his first appearance at her father's court in disguise, in the role of a simple young pupil of the great painter. A serenade, composed by him, is still sung in Leuchtenstein and Babenhausen. Of these things I can tell you nothing with certainty, they shall be left to the imagination of romantic persons.

Be this as it may, the young princely worshipper of the Muses returned to his own court, craving nothing in the world but to marry Princess Ludmilla of Leuchtenstein.

The ceremonial demand in marriage was made and accepted. And on a bright October day, when the vintage was just finished, the city of Babenhausen welcomed its young Princess. Fresh and pure as a peony bud, tender and playful as a child, the bride made the loyal Babenhauseners scatter their very hearts with the rain of flowers upon the pavement before her coach.

A row of brilliant balls, banquets and gala performances ensued. The whole court was smiling, and old chamberlains with tears in their eyes witnessed the display of princely matrimonial happiness.

The young couple, like two instruments of different nature, melted together in melodious happiness. Princess Ludmilla, delighted to delight, led the dance, and Prince Lothar, still wooing what he had won, followed his young wife through all its figures. The Grand Duchess looked on and smiled. The glory of the house of Fugger-Babenhausen was to be maintained.

It was and it was not. On a day shortly before Christmas Prince Lothar came to see his mother and calmly and candidly, as he did everything, informed her that the Ducal heir, on whom her mind and heart had for so long been concentrating, was about to make his entry in the world a full two months before law and decency permitted.

The Grand Duchess was struck dumb, first with amazement, for she had never imagined the possibility of such a thing in *bonne compagnie*. Then with horror, for what would the nation think of a scandal in the ruling house—what, in particular, would the dubious branch of the house itself think, and make, of it? In the end with terrible wrath against her son. And with this last emotion came a crushing feeling of guilt. For had she not herself delivered her frail child into the hands of that demonic figure, Herr Cazotte, and had not Herr Cazotte, talking about Lothar, pronounced the sentence: "With him the idea is action." The Grand Duchess trembled.

The next moment she was folded in the arms of the miscreant himself. And in this embrace, the first that her son had ever offered her on his own accord, her whole being melted. The world was changed round her, slowly, like a landscape at sunrise, it filled with new surprising tinges of tenderness and rapture. And this, I may here state, was the first triumph of the cherubic child upon whose small figure so much of my tale does turn.

Before she had spoken a word the Grand Duchess had determined to side with her son and daughter-in-law. She would keep their secret even from her husband. She took no further decision at the moment, but when Prince Lothar had left her and she was again alone, she realized that a line of action would have to be found.

To her own surprise the Grand Duchess at once found herself longing for Herr Cazotte. The tail and cloven hoof of the gentleman faded out of the picture, she recalled his second remark about Lothar ("And with him the action is idea") and smiled.

But Herr Cazotte was away in Rome, painting the portrait of Cardinal Salviati. So the Grand Duchess spent the strangest Christmas of her life, with a dimly radiant Christmas tree somewhere in front of her and parcels of secrets in her drawers.

However, between Christmas and the New Year an event took place which gave her a kind of respite. On a sledge party in the mountains the two panached horses before the young princely couple's sledge shied at an old woman carrying wood, ran away and upset the sledge in a deep drift of snow. None of the passengers came to any harm, Princess Ludmilla's rosy face laughed up at her rescuers. But her mother-in-law was alarmed, she sent for the old physician-in-ordinary, Professor Putziger, and told him everything. Professor Putziger ordered his patient to stay in bed for three weeks; for that length of time the Grand Duchess felt a kind of safety.

A fortnight later Herr Cazotte returned from Rome, pleased with his portrait. The Grand Duchess at once sent for him. Although she felt it beneath her to lay any responsibility on him, the artist realized that he was here being taken to task as a person at home in the land of romance and as Prince Lothar's guide and mentor in it.

"Madame," said Herr Cazotte, "The Lord God, that great artist, at times paints his pictures in such a manner as to be best appreciated at a long distance. A hundred and fifty years hence your present predicament will have all the look of an idyll composed to delight its spectators. Your difficulty at this moment is that you are a little too close to it."

"I am very close to it, *mon ami*," said the Grand Duchess.

"Each of your loyal subjects," said Herr Cazotte, "did he know of the matter which now vexes you, would smile in his heart, for all the world loves a lover. At the same time he might feel it his duty to pull a grave face. You are feeling and behaving just like him, Madame. Do not let your own face deceive you."

"But what are we to *do?*" asked the Grand Duchess.

"Providence," said Herr Cazotte, "has stepped in to help us. We must not fall out of step with it."

He developed to the Grand Duchess a plan which, although it must have been conceived on the spot, seemed well thought through.

The Grand Duke and the nation of Babenhausen, he pronounced, would be informed, quite truthfully, that a hope for the dynasty was dawning. The date for the happy event, in the announcement to them, would be put down for the middle of July. They would further be informed that upon Professor Putziger's advice the Princess should keep to her bed for three months, and that even after that period she would have to live in utmost seclusion.

During these three months a country resort must be found, everything in it arranged as comfortably and harmoniously as possible, and a small trustworthy court formed. In April the precious patient would be escorted, with care, to the chosen residence and there, in the middle of May, the infant would actually be born.

It was upon the subsequent two months that the whole matter turned. That period alone would be really perilous, and the partisans of the rightful Grand Ducal house were here called upon to form as a stone wall of loyal hearts round an exalted secret. At the end of it, on the fifteenth of July, a cannonade—the cannonade, it was to be hoped, of a hundred and one guns announcing the birth of a male heir—from the old citadel of Babenhausen would proclaim to town and country the great and happy news.

Certainly one would have to be careful even after that date. The traditional pompous baptism must be held within a few weeks. Here it was a lucky thing that the old Archbishop was extremely short-sighted. After this great event the young princely couple might quite naturally take up their summer residence for the rest of the season. And about the end of September the proud Babenhauseners would be pluming themselves on their lusty and clever little Prince.

The Grand Duchess went through the plan carefully and approved of it. In further meetings between her and Herr Cazotte, at times joined by the young father-to-be, it was built up in detail.

The choice of the residence itself was entrusted to Herr Cazotte. After various expeditions this gentleman for Princess Ludmilla's place of confinement picked out the little chateau of Rosenbad, a rococo hermitage, charmingly situated on a mountain slope by a lake and among woods, and isolated from the rest of the world. For a month he devoted all his talents to fitting out and furnishing the place.

Next a list of the members of the small court was drawn up. Old Professor Putziger as a matter of course would be staying at the chateau in constant attention to the Princess. A distinguished *Oberhofmeisterin* was found in the Countess Poggendorff, who twenty-five years before had been maid-of-honor to the Grand Duchess herself. The Grand Duchess' old maid and valet were transferred from her service to that of her daughter-in-law. The roll was lengthening sweetly.

The Grand Duchess, participating in an intrigue, was rejuvenated by thirty years. She might to the one side partake of her consort's legitimate dynastic gratification, while to the other she kept herself pleasantly occupied by little tête-a-têtes with Herr Cazotte. She even undertook two trips to Schloss Rosenbad.

A problem presented itself with the nomination of a maid-of-honor to the Princess. The present one was not, to the mind of the Grand Duchess, all that could be desired, for she had three married sisters at court, all three notable gossips. The question when gone into proved more difficult than first assumed, for the young lady who was to hold the office would have to be of such birth, education and appearance as would to the eyes of the world justify her election. She would furthermore have to be young and sweet-tempered, since the Princess in her seclusion would want a companion of her own age and temperament. And where does one, these days, find a pleasant young girl of the highest society with the elevation of mind, the steadfastness of character and the unwavering loyalty of heart demanded by the situation? Tell me that, my dear Herr Cazotte!

Herr Cazotte sat for some time in silence with a thoughtful face. Possibly he had already made his choice, but was taking pleasure in letting the highborn maidens of Babenhausen pass muster before his inner eye.

In the end he said: "Ehrengard von Schreckenstein."

"Schreckenstein?" the Grand Duchess asked. "The daughter of that General von Schreckenstein who was my father-in-law's aide-de-camp?"

"The same," said Herr Cazotte.

"But my dear Herr Cazotte," the Grand

Duchess exclaimed after a moment. "The Schreckensteins are Lutherans!"

"They are?" said the painter, as if pleasantly surprised.

"One of the few old Lutheran families of the country," said the lady. "A very stern, indeed puritan breed. All military people."

"A most fortunate coincidence," said Herr Cazotte. "If the Roman Catholic mind has a greater picturesqueness, the Lutheran mind has a steelier armature—an armature, Madame, being that iron skeleton round which the sculptor builds up his clay."

"The General," said the Grand Duchess, "was first married to a von Kniphausen and by her had five sons, all in the army. Then later in life he married a Solenhofen-Puechau and by his second wife had this daughter. Where have you seen the girl? I seem to remember her now," she added. "Nothing much to look at."

"O Madame," said Herr Cazotte. "Speak not so. She has been presented at Court, and I have seen her. In a white frock. A young

Walkyrie. Brought up in the sternest military virtues, in the vast and grim castle of Schreckenstein, the only daughter of a warrior clan. An almost unbelievably fitting white-hot young angel with a flaming sword to stand sentinel before our young lovers' paradise!"

"*Gauche*," said the Grand Duchess thoughtfully.

"Young," Herr Cazotte agreed. "Long-legged. With big hands and a forehead like a Nike."

"I have been told, I think," the Grand Duchess remarked, "that the Schreckenstein girl is to marry her cousin, a von Blittersdorff, of my guards. Or that, although there be no official engagement, the marriage for a long time has been agreed upon by the families. Will not the girl blab in her letters to her fiancé?"

"Unless the young guardsman's birthday falls within our particular two months," Herr Cazotte answered, "I doubt whether the young lady will be writing him any letters at all. The Schreckensteins are not a literary family."

"I shall think the matter over," said the

Grand Duchess. "For mind you, this is a very important post on our list."

"The most important of all," said Herr Cazotte, "with the exception of one. Of that of a gentleman with sufficient knowledge of the world, and with sufficient deadly devotion to the house of Fugger-Babenhausen, to act as liaison officer and to be moving freely between the outside world and the enchanted castle. Him it may take us some time and trouble to find."

"That gentleman," said the Grand Duchess, "has already been found and already been appointed." With these words she gracefully gave Herr Cazotte her hand to kiss.

The great lady, after having thought the matter over, had an interview with General von Schreckenstein.

This gray-haired warrior, inflexible in his military doctrines, held vaguer views on sentimental matters, the which he took to be mainly women's domain. He listened to the flattering confidential princely communication and made no questions. The situation, he gathered, would involve no trifling with the sacred, fundamental principle of legitimacy. And no Schreckenstein had ever failed in loyalty to his Sovereign. He would, he said, inform and instruct his daughter.

Herr Cazotte himself later paid a visit to the castle of Schreckenstein. He was familiar with the plan and the history of the place and enchanted with its medieval ramparts and dungeons. He also enjoyed General von Schreckenstein's complete ignorance of his own name and work.

So the name of Ehrengard von Schreckenstein was entered into the Grand Duchess' list of the Schloss Rosenbad household.

❧

And with this settlement, my dears, the prelude to, or the first movement of my little story terminates. I shall name it "Prince Lothar." Now, entering upon the next chapter of the tale, we are moving from the town to the country, into the peaceful setting of big trees, clear lakes and grassy slopes. My second movement is a pastorale, and shall be named "Rosenbad."

Herr Cazotte in the last week of April wrote to my great-grandmother:

My Dearest Friend and Benefactress,

You ask me for a description of Schloss Rosenbad. Imagine to yourself that you be quietly stepping into a painting by Claude Lorrain, and that the landscape around you becomes alive, balsamic breezes wafting and violets turning the mountain sides into long gentle waves of blue! And imagine, in the midst of this delightful scenery, our small scene and temple of delight. You may mount the stairs at liberty and walk undisturbed from room to room: an artist and poet, you will then admit, has gone through the house before you and has made it speak.

You have seldom seen me satisfied with my own work, and often distressed by my own worthlessness. Do not, now, shake your head at my outburst of triumph. The triumph is not mine, and I take no credit for it. I am in service, "Ich dien."

The Goddess of Love, the Lady Venus herself, has entrusted me with the work, and I have only followed her instructions. In the landscape, the light, the season and the situation itself she has whispered to me and ordered me to re-erect, in the blue mountains, her ancient, sunken and slandered residence: the Venusberg.

How hard and happily I have worked in her employ. I have succeeded in preserving the charm of remoteness, reverie and decay of the place, and I have polished it, upholstered it in silk and colored it in tints of rose, making of it a nest of classic elegance and comfort. Look up and down, right and left, with your most critical eye—you will not find a single tone which be not harmoniously tuned into the harmony of the whole. Voluptuousness breathes through the rooms, stairs and corridors, voluptuousness lingers in the folds of the curtains and smilingly gazes at you from the tapestries on the walls. In these surroundings our young Princess cannot fail to give birth to an amorino.

I am holding a privileged post at the Venusberg Court as mediator between Rosenbad and Babenhausen. And what a happy côterie we form inside the magic ring! A particular charm is given to our daily life by the fact that our circle has had to be restricted to a minimum. We are gardeners and milkmaids, grooms and waiters in the service of the seaborn Goddess. I myself, as you know, am a fairly skilled chef and do often give a hand to old François.

The good Babenhauseners turn their eyes towards the Venusberg with loyal approval and hope, discussing the bulletins. We are silent, mentally each of us has a finger on the lips. But through our silence ripples of smiles are running. At times I hear the drops of the Venetian chandeliers jingling with subdued laughter and the jets of the garden fountains joining in.

Is not your boudoir as you open this letter filled with fragrance?

Your most deeply devoted
Cazotte

P.S. Walking in the garden this evening Prince Lothar said to Princess Ludmilla: "So here is Paradise." And with her head upon his shoulder his young wife echoed: "Paradise." I smiled benevolence on them, like an archangel assisting the Lord in laying out the garden of Eden, and smiling on the first human male and female. But the great landscape architect himself, when his work had been completed, on looking at it and listening to the Gloria and Hallelujah of his angelic chorus, will have felt the craving for a clear, unbiased eye to view it with him, the eye of a critic, a connoisseur and an arbiter. With what creature, in all Paradise, will he have found that eye, Madame? Madame— with the Serpent!

Your obedient servant, etc.

On the first of May he again wrote:

I saw, at a court ball, a girl in a white frock, the daughter of warriors, in whose universe art, or the artist, have never existed. And I cried with Michelangelo: "My greatest triumph hides within that block of marble."

Since then I have at times ventured to believe that it be this vision of mine which has caused our entire course of events and has, in the end, lifted my young eaglet off her native mountain peak to drop her in the flower garden of Rosenbad.

What will be now, to the true artist, the fine fleur of her being? In what act is a nature like hers, within the chosen moment, to give forth itself most exhaustively? I have pictured her in every possible situation and posture, in itself a sweet pursuit.

And I made my decision. In the blush.

You will not, I know, for a moment be thinking of the blush of offended modesty which might be called forth, from the outside, by a coarse and blunt assailant, if one coarse and blunt enough could be found. To the mind of the artist the very idea is blasphemy, he turns away his face from it. You will no more be thinking of the blush of anger, the which, from the outside, I myself —preserve me—might bring about. None of the two would, in any case, be what I want. Events from outside will, by law of nature, come to Ehrengard and will mean nothing at all to her. She will marry—and I do not envy the man who is to enter into relationship with the Schreckensteins, personally I should prefer to enter their dungeon—she will bear ten soldier sons, and it will mean nothing at all to her. What is really to happen to this admirable, this unique nature is to happen within herself.

So I shall in time be drawing my young Amazon's blood, not down onto the ground —for I dislike the sight of human blood outside the human body, it is the wrong color and mars a picture—but upwards from the deepest, most secret and sacred wells of her being, making it cover her all over like a transparent crimson veil and making it burn her up in one single exquisite gasp of flame.

If I have succeeded in placing her in surroundings and in a situation which might bring a blush to the cheek of another virgin, I do by no means wish her to blush in reluctance to, or from fear of, the perils round her. No, her blood is to rise, in pride and amour-propre, in unconditional surrender to those perils, in the enraptured flinging over of her entire being to the powers which, till this hour, with her entire being she has rejected and denied, in full, triumphant consent to her own perdition. In this blush her past, present, and future will be thrown before my feet. She is to be the rose which drops every one of her petals to one single breath of the wind and stands bared.

In high mountains, as you will know, there exists a phenomenon of nature called Alpen-Glühen.

Scientists will tell us that it is caused by a rare play of the spectral colors in the atmosphere, to the looker-on it is a miracle.

After the sun has set, and as the whole majestic mountain landscape is already withdrawing into itself, suddenly the row of summits, all on their own, radiate a divine fire, a celestial, deep rose flame, as if they were giving up a long kept secret. After that they disappear, nothing more dramatic can be imagined: they have betrayed their inmost substance and can now only annihilate themselves. Black night follows.

Tall white-clad mountains will naturally be a little slow in the uptake, but when at last they do realize and conceive, what glow, you heavens, and what glorification. And what void afterwards.

I have seen the Alpen-Glühen once, the moment is among the greatest of my existence, and when it was over I said to myself that I would give ten years of my life to see this once more. And yet after all it has been but a presage of my adventure with Ehrengard.

Your obedient servant, etc.

Cazotte

Princess Ludmilla was exceedingly happy at Schloss Rosenbad.

She was delighted to be out of bed, in the open air and country and in the company of people with whom she could speak openly. She felt affectionately towards each member of her small court.

Herr Cazotte, in the center of it, by now was an old friend. He played the piano to her French and Italian songs; entertained her with gossip and anecdotes; when she had no appetite he concocted with his own hands marvelous cosmopolitan dishes; and from his visits to town brought back fine old lace for the dainty princely cradle.

Countess Poggendorff, the *Oberhof-meisterin*, encompassed her young mistress with graceful attention. From the coquettish lace cap on her head to the tip of her dainty shoe, the tiniest lady's shoe in Babenhausen and a bit smaller than her foot, she was an emotionalist, and impressionable like a girl of fifteen. Once again within romantic surroundings and in an atmosphere of passion and danger she saw her own youth revived, charmed everybody and radiated a *languissant* benevolence on the household.

And as far as Princess Ludmilla's relations with her new young maid-of-honor were concerned, the Princess, heavy with the sweetness of life, like a bee on its way home to the hive, was unable to see in her companion anything less than a sister. When the two girls slowly made the round of the rose garden, Ludmilla, who was the younger and smaller, would lean on Ehrengard's shoulder, but how infinitely wiser and more experienced, how much the elder sister did she not feel the while. At times she was almost afraid to display her immense superiority, she would then become more tender in her manner and would only reveal her advantage in a kind of tender raillery.

She was intrigued by Ehrengard's lonely life at the Schreckenstein castle, asked her questions about her five tall brothers, whom she had seen at court, and shuddered at the description of the blizzards in the mountains and the ghosts in the old gray block of stones. She was keen to learn about her friend's handsome young fiancé and his courtship. Ehrengard, in order to supply the information expected from her, had to think a good deal more about Kurt von

Blittersdorff than till now she had ever done. Kurt, she informed the Princess, had fought several duels.

"But were you not terrified then, beside yourself with fear and grief?" Ludmilla asked.

"Kurt is a very good swordsman," Ehrengard replied. "He has taught me to fence too."

"Have you kissed him, Ehrengard?" Ludmilla enquired after one of her long pauses.

"Yes, I have kissed him many times when we were children," said Ehrengard. "He is my cousin. While he was at school he used to stay at Schreckenstein during his holidays."

After another pause Ludmilla asked: "Have you two ever had a secret together?"

"Yes," Ehrengard again answered. "When the boys had done something bad, and I helped them to keep it from Papa."

The Princess was silent, then suddenly exclaimed in a low voice: "Try to have a secret with him. Something that, in the whole world, only you and he know of. You will be feeling, then, that he is you and you are he."

Herr Cazotte wrote:

Ehrengard—like, I believe, most people of severely moral milieus—is not aware that she has learned any principles, and indeed does not know the meaning of the word principle. Her moral code she takes to be a codex of laws of nature, the which you need not explain or uphold since they will explain and uphold themselves.

She is a country-bred girl, and familiar with the facts of life. She knows at what date after the wedding a child should be born. With servant girls of Schreckenstein irregularities have occurred, she has watched the abhorrence and wrath in faces of old housekeepers and governesses, and to her, then, as by the very law of gravitation, the girl in question has been a fallen woman. But inasmuch as the one fundamental law of her own nature is the loyalty of the house of Schreckenstein to the house of Fugger-Babenhausen, in present circumstances the reversion of the rule is legal and logical. A moral volte-face of this kind might be difficult to an old trained casuist, but a young girl will accomplish it with a high hand.

The paradox of our relationship is therefore this: that while I am making her drink in by eye, ear, and nostril and by every pore of her clear skin the sweet poison of the Venusberg, it is I who am, in reality, teaching her and impressing upon her the nature and the necessity of moral principle. When she has fully appropriated the nature of principles and the necessity to herself of principles, then I am victorious, then the moment of my triumph has come.

In the meantime I am enjoying every mien and movement of my youthful victim. It has taken five hundred years of isolation, discipline, and consciousness of absolute power, and of total abstinence from and ignorance of the arts, to make these. A wild animal, when it believes itself unobserved, moves and gazes about in that same way. Diana once walked through the woods of

*Arcady like that. At the same time she is, as
the Grand Duchess pronounced, gauche.*

Of an evening, while the Princess rested
on her sofa, Prince Lothar would play chess
with Ehrengard. To him the chessboard was a
deeply fascinating symbol of life and worthy of
his entire attention. Ehrengard had been taught
the game by General von Schreckenstein who,
by now cut off from actual military exertion,
still liked to practice his strategic skill and to
operate with cavalry, artillery and infantry.

Herr Cazotte wrote:

*In many ways—although without pos-
sessing his talents or his sentiment—she is so
much like the Prince that the two might well
be brother and sister. When I spoke to the
Grand Duchess of plastic unity of being, I
might have been discussing the maid-of-
honor. Both are strikingly straight and well-
balanced. But while the balance of my young
lord is heaven-aspiring, like that of a young
tree striving towards zenith, the girl is bal-*

anced to perfection in the manner of those little toy figures with lead at the base of them, which cannot be overturned.

Prince Lothar was an eager horseman as well, and in the beginning of May, when to all sides and in every way the landscape was getting lovelier, he invited his wife's maid-of-honor to accompany him on his rides. At times Herr Cazotte would join them.

Herr Cazotte wrote:

Ehrengard has found the horses of our Rosenbad stables too sedate for her taste, and has asked to have her own mount brought from Schreckenstein. It is a fine and fiery black horse named Wotan, hard for anybody to manage but its young mistress herself. When those two lead the way, we are all making light of hurdles or ditches. My Lord Lothar admires Ehrengard as a fearless horsewoman. I myself wonder whether the reckless rides be not unconscious attempts at escape. She is getting uneasy in the heavily-scented air of Rosenbad and begins to find it difficult to draw her breath in it. Her whole vigorous youthful constitution cries out for strong exercise. My gallant Ehrengard! You would never consent to run away from a danger. Set your mind at rest, from your present danger you cannot run away.

On the eighth of May a little Prince was born at Schloss Rosenbad.

As the first shrill, preternatural cry rang from the Princess' room round which the household had been listening, the chateau trembled and was changed from cellar to attics. A sigh of happy relief ran through all rooms. But in the very next instant the silence became infinitely deeper and more momentous. Who would have the heart to betray the tiny defenseless newcomer? Death to each inhabitant of the house would be preferable.

A lovelier child had never seen the light of day in Babenhausen. Professor Putziger himself was surprised at the faultlessness of the infant and put on an additional pair of glasses to exmine it. The trusted midwife, who had once helped Prince Lothar into the world, was bound to admit that the son outshone the father. Countess Poggendorff cooed before the cradle: "*L'on se sent plus belle devant une telle beauté! L'on se sent plus innocente devant une telle innocence!*" From the silky topknot to the rosy toenails the baby was perfection.

A courier was at once dispatched to the Grand Duchess. The poor lady, for fear of publicity, had not dared to break off her stay with the Grand Duke at their usual watering place. She had passed the last weeks in a state of great nervous excitement by the side of her unsuspecting husband. Her sudden outburst of tears at the apparently insignificant tidings from Rosenbad, as a sign of unwonted weakness in his consort, made the Grand Duke resolve to prolong their sojourn at the bath.

A new figure, of great importance in the household as well as in this story, now made her appearance in the Rosenbad circle. Her name was Lispeth. Magnificently dressed in the costume of the province, with embroidered cambric and long silk ribbons, she was a pleasant sight, big and buxom, pink and white, with a round, gentle and genial face. She was the daughter and granddaughter of faithful gamekeepers to the Grand Ducal house, and already some time ago had been picked out by the Grand Duchess and Professor Putziger, with the utmost regard to physical and moral qualities, as nurse to its small hope.

The young mother, in the satin and lace of her four-poster, at the first sight of the young peasant woman had shed a few tears of jealousy. But she was soon won over to see her rival as a kind of second self, stronger and wiser and with more knowledge of life, for Lispeth had got two children beside the baby which she had left in order to give her warm bosom and heart to the little Prince, an arbiter and oracle in all vital matters. Her privileged position was acknowledged in the house, Countess Poggendorff and Herr Cazotte took trouble to ingratiate themselves with the country woman who spoke the strong dialect of the province.

The problem of the baby's christening had

now to be settled. The great ceremony within the cathedral of Babenhausen would be taking place towards the end of July. How then were things to be managed during the interval of ten weeks? To have a child christened twice is blasphemy. Yet could his devotees consent to expose their precious charge to any bodily or spiritual risks by leaving him unbaptized for that length of time? Lispeth took her place on the council as an expert on changelings and oafs. Steel, she declared, must always be kept in the cradle, rats or mice must not be mentioned, yarn must not be wound, and by no means must the name of the Devil be as much as whispered inside the walls of the chateau. Herr Cazotte, himself being a son of the people, enjoined all these precautionary measures.

Herr Cazotte wrote:

Ehrengard undoubtedly for the first time in her life and without knowing it herself, as altogether she knows very little about herself, has fallen in love. It will serve my purpose. To fall in love with the God of Love himself may well be, to a mind of her energy and collectedness, the first step towards a deeper, final fall. The guileless figure of Cupid, the embodiment of love, himself ignorant of and immune to the passion, is the most fatal of dolls. I have sometimes wondered at seeing mothers placidly encouraging their small daughters to play with dolls. A little girl is a deep creature and may by instinct know more about the facts of life than the elderly maiden governess who teaches her her ABC's. And while the Mama is looking to the future and reasoning that to her daughter the moment of supreme sacrifice will be lying a full fifteen years ahead, the daughter with her delicate roots in the dark mould of the past will be aware of that supreme moment of her existence, lying only five or six years back.

My young lady of Schreckenstein till now has taken no interest in infants. She has, she tells me, got nephews, but she has seen little of them and does, I understand, view them mainly as generals-to-be. The pathetic gracefulness of a baby to her is a new and surprising phenomenon. She does not smile and sigh over the little Prince as does our sweet Madame Poggendorff, she stands up straight by the cradle side, lost in contemplation. Once, as his nurse held him up, I saw her slowly raising his hand to her lips and passing the small fingers over them one by one, thoughtfully, as if a little alarmed by the softness and smoothness of the skin.

Am I jealous? By no means. I take it as a pretty compliment on the part of the God of Love that he should call, in the flesh, on his devoted priest.

Now that the maid-of-honor was partly relieved of her duty as companion to her mistress, she did not always know what to do with herself at Rosenbad and welcomed Herr Cazotte's conversation. It even became obvious to the small court that she preferred his company to that of others and would look round for him if she did not find him in the room or on the terrace.

The great artist was gentle and courteous, if a little impersonal, in his manner with the highborn maiden. From his rich treasury of knowledge he took out for her benefit strange tales of ancient times, theories of art and life and fancies of his own on the phenomena of existence. He entertained her, too, with narrations of his own eventful life, dwelling on the days when he was a poor boy in shabby clothes, or slightly touching on his triumphs at academies and courts, and sprinkling his talk with accounts of the life of outcasts in dark streets or with bits of scandal from sublime places.

He found that the girl had read little and lent her books from his exclusive library or read out to her in the shade of the big trees. Poetry, new to her, puzzled and fascinated her. Herr Cazotte had a voice made for reciting poetry and had often been asked to read by princesses and *beaux-esprits*. At times he would lower the book with a finger in it and go on reciting with his eyes in the tree crowns.

On a very lovely evening he had been reading to her in the garden and was slowly accompanying her back to the house, when he stopped and made her stop with him by a fountain representing Leda and the swan and repeated a stanza from the poem they had last read together. He was silent for a while, the girl was silent with him, and as he turned toward her he found her young face very still.

"A penny for your thoughts, my Lady Ehrengard," he said.

She looked at him, and for a moment a very slight blush slid over her face.

"I was not," after a pause she answered him slowly and gravely, "really thinking of anything at all."

He had no doubt that here, as ever, she was speaking the truth.

Herr Cazotte wrote:

You smile, dear friend, at my complaints that Ehrengard occupies my mind too much and is monopolizing it to such an extent that I am in sheer self-preservation longing for the moment when I shall have done with her and be free to take up other interests in life. And although you be the glass of matronly virtue to all Babenhausen, you will be asking in your heart: "Why does not the silly fool seduce the girl in the orthodox and old-fashioned manner and set his mind at rest?" My answer to your question is: "Madame, the silly fool is an artist."

He is at this moment an artist absorbed in and intoxicated by the creation of his chef d'oeuvre. Food and rest are nothing to him, he is fed by winged inspiration as the Prophet Elijah was fed by his ravens. Allow me to let you participate in the working of an artist's mind.

I insist on obtaining a full surrender without any physical touch whatever. I kiss the hands of our married ladies and have respectfully placed a kiss or two on Mistress Lispeth's broad brown hand, while I have hardly brushed with my own Ehrengard's slender, strong fingers. But how resolutely do not the hands of my mind caress every part of hers, how insistingly run over the inmost strings of her being, tuning them to

wheel from them their deepest sounds and vi-
brations.

I might, upon your friendly advice, un-
dertake to seduce the girl in the orthodox and
old-fashioned manner, and the task might
not be as difficult as it looks. All marble she is
not; were she so, she would not interest me.
She has within her fire enough for an artillery
charge and warmth enough for a cow house,
the Schreckensteins having been, for five hundred years, both condottieri and cattlemen. I
might seduce her, for she is impulsive and
unreflecting, in a particularly impetuous moment of hers. And, Madame, it would mean
nothing.

For her ruin, in such a case, would be a
fact and a reality. And she knows about facts
and realities—as the daughter of a long line
of men of action she very likely knows more
about them than your humble servant. She
might, in such a case, save herself by some
real and actual measure. She might well, in
one single, deadly collected movement, re-
nounce the world and retire to desiccate, a

dumb, tall mummy on horseback, upon her mountain. Or she might seize upon the idea of revenge and rouse her brothers and her young fiancé to kill me, a very brutal end to an artistic enterprise.

Set your mind at rest. She is safe within my hands and will be more thoroughly seduced than was ever any other maiden.

Pious people tell us that our moments of earthly delight be but echoes of a former, heavenly existence. I believe them. It will be so with Ehrengard von Schreckenstein when I have accomplished my task. From the moment when, in deep gratitude, I have bared my head to her and left her, any touch of physical delight within her life to her will be but the echo of my celestial embrace.

How will she, then, save herself? To the world I have never in the least compromised her, yet she will know herself to be ultimately and hopelessly compromised. The world did not grudge sweet Gretchen—the heroine of my gigantic namesake—her guilt, it admitted her crime of infanticide and her debt to the sword of justice. To that same world Ehrengard will still be on her pedestal, the snow-white virgin, and yet she will know herself just as clearly as Gretchen to be fallen, broken and lost. Will she not then, in her turn, in sheer self-preservation, be dependent on me as the one and only confirmer of her perdition, the unique guarantor of the loss, the blowing up of her virginity? Will she not for the rest of her life be dragging herself after me, wringing her hands, crying out my name incessantly, regularly, with the might of all the clocks of Babenhausen? Alas, Madame, she will not catch me up, for I shall be away painting other fair ladies, having handed her over, intact but annihilated, to the fond cares of a young husband who will never have the faintest notion that he is drinking up my remains.

And will not then, you ask me, her ruin be a fact and a reality? Verily, my friend, it will be so, inasmuch as the reality of Art be superior to that of the material world. Inasmuch as the artist be, everywhere and at all times, the arbiter on reality.

I have, on a trip to town, taken the trouble to look up our young guardsman. He is, by the way, shortly coming up to this neighborhood for the big maneuvers, but will naturally have no chance of recalling himself to his fiancée. I have found him to be all that I can desire for the role of a spiritual cuckold.

My heart kisses your hand.

Cazotte

P.S. Why should I not confide to you a fancy of mine which much occupied my thoughts at the time when I was a small lonely boy bewildered in existence, at the time before I met you? As you have been aware, I have never known the name of my father. Still, a father I will have had, and I thank him for contributing to giving me eyes, ears and a nose with which to enjoy the world. The little street Arab of Babenhausen took in, transported, the sights, sounds and smells round

him. He was deeply in love with color and
brilliancy and would follow the soldiers and
the dashing officers in the streets, dwelling
on the idea that one of these were his father.
Now when in the early spring I visited the
Schreckenstein castle this long-forgotten
whim suddenly came back to me: why should
not that imposing figure, General Schreckenstein, be my papa? We are alike in many
ways. I, too, have got small ears set close to
the head, and I, too, am fearless by nature.
The General as a young guardsman will have
had his amourettes in garrison towns, and to
seduce and abandon a housemaid to him will
have seemed a matter of no consequence. Yet
the order of the Universe is sublime, graceful and inexorable. Inside it nothing is without a consequence, but your first move on the
board may in the end pronounce you mate.
A thoughtless move on the first night of July
—for I was born, as all through our acquaint-
ance you have been kind enough to remember, on the first of April, a true and guaran-
teed fool—may snow you under, finally, in

your gala uniform and decorations and your
towering castle. Unwillingly the father initi-
ates the son into the law that things have got
consequences, that even a case of seduction
will have them, and the initiated brother
passes on the knowledge to his young sister.

And what lofty spiritual heavenly court
of justice will pass sentence on my case of
lofty, spiritual, heavenly incest?

It was a kind of rite in the life of Herr
Cazotte that he should pass the first night of
July out-of-doors. Faithful to it, on that same
night, shortly after the court and the household
of Rosenbad had gone to bed, he walked out
below pale stars in a pale sky, in a world drip-
ping with dew and filled with fragrance. He
first walked quickly to get away, then slowed
down to gaze round him. As he did so his heart
overflowed with gratitude. He took off his hat.

"What tremendous, unfathomable power
of imagination," he said to himself, "has formed
each of the smallest details here, and combined
them into a mighty unity. I am no modest per-

son, I think pretty highly of my own talents, and I venture to believe that I might have imagined one or the other of the things that surround me. I might have invented the long grass—but could I have invented the dew? I might have invented the dusk, but could I have invented the stars? I know," he said to himself as he stood quite still and listened, "that I could not have invented the nightingale.

"The blossoms of the chestnut tree," he went on, "hold themselves up straight like altar candles. The blossoms of the lilac seem to be rushing in all directions from the stem and the branches, making of the whole bush an exuberant bouquet, the flowers of the laburnum drop like golden summer icicles in the pale blue air. But the blossoms of the hawthorn lie along the branches like light layers of white and rosy snow. Such infinite variance cannot possibly be necessitated by the economy of Nature, it will needs be the manifestation of a universal spirit—inventive, buoyant and frolicsome to excess, incapable of holding back is playful torrents of bliss. Indeed, indeed: *Domine, non sum dignus.*"

He strolled for a long time through the woods. "I am tonight," he thought, "paying my respects to the great god Pan."

The summer night lightened round him, the colors began to come out, tardily, as if reluctantly, in the grass and the trees. The wanderer's trouser legs were soaked high above his knees and set with burrs and thorns. In his pocket he had a round of bread and a slice of cheese, and he now sat down on the grassy slope of a small clear mountain brook to eat it, washing it down with ice-cold water from a small tin cup. Herr Cazotte, as far as food and drink went, was an ascetic. In his very young days he had been so from necessity, later, although he could value meat and wine to a nicety, by inclination, today he was keeping up the habit in order to preserve his figure. His simple meal finished, he leaned his back to a willow tree, and for a long time sat immovable, from the depth of his heart applauding the universe.

"And even little Johann Wolfgang Cazotte," he thought, "has been fitted in very prettily and is indeed at the moment indispensable to the mighty whole. As what?" After a pause he answered himself: "As a small, innocent and happy, wet and dirty satyr in the big dark woods."

He got up and started walking back. He had promised to assist Princess Ludmilla with the program for a little musical soirée, a surprise for Prince Lothar upon the anniversary of their first meeting. He was a punctual person, and as he walked he looked at his watch; he had plenty of time.

His path ran along the mountain lake. From time to time he stopped to let his eyes caress the landscape and his nose draw in the pure air. His walk would soon be over, and he would once more from the melodious solitude of the wood and the slope be back in the company of human beings who did not always understand him. He had sharp ears, and now he heard voices not far off, low, clear women's voices. He left the path and made his way through the shrubbery to get a view of the speakers.

Now, twenty feet away, somewhat below him where the lake narrowed and ended up, a couple of stone steps had been built into the green slope; here one could land a boat. Upon the steps were two female figures, in whom after a minute he recognized Ehrengard and her maid. Ehrengard was undressing, and the maid picking up and folding her garments. Just as he looked at her she let her shift drop to the ground and stood for a moment all naked, very quiet, gazing round.

Above the water sheet the haze was lifting like delicate layers of veils being withdrawn one by one. In the light of the coming sunrise it was roseate and opalescent, less white than the girl's body, the thin streamers clinging to her foot and knee like a lastly-shed, cobwebby garment. She stepped forth amid it, slender, strong, her head raised, her long tresses gathered together above it in a crescent. The maid collected her clothes and retired with them to the grass. The young girl seemed to be the only human being between the clear water and the clear sky. The trees and rushes were all her friends and playmates, unobserved like herself. She hesitated for a moment with one slim foot in the water, then went in, gently breaking its surface as she let it rise to her knee, bosom and shoulders. A little way out she stopped and lifted her arms to bind her hair tighter, as she got in deeper she filled her hands to bathe her face. She lingered in the water, moving slowly, a water nymph happily back in her element.

After a while she again ascended from the embrace of the lake. Her perfect solitude was broken as her maid came out from the bushes to wrap a big towel round her and, lowly chattering and chuckling, to rub her dry. Together they disappeared from view behind the shrub, their voices were still heard for a moment or two, then everything was silent once more, they had gone away.

Herr Cazotte became very grave. While watching the vision before him he had thought of nothing at all, his soul had been in his eyes. As now, slowly, he let notions and ideas come back to him, he realized that here he had been, as never before, elected and favored, overwhelmed with grace.

A unique motif had been granted to a

great artist, that was one thing. He had proved himself to be right, and more than right, in his valuation of the girl's beauty, that was another.

But the generosity of the Gods was more alarming and astounding still.

For their gift to him was of a direct and personal nature, the immortal powers had consented to cooperate with him in the purpose which had so long held him. Frolicsome they were, hilarious and magnanimous to excess. And dangerous, dangerous for a mortal, even for an artist, to associate with. He became still graver.

She would come back, of that he was certain. The Gods would not cheat him. Probably her early morning bathing in the lake was a recurrent event and a daily observance, which she was keeping secret to all the world with the exception of her maid.

The picture which he had here been ordered to paint—"Nymph bathing in a forest lake," or "The bath of Diana"—would be in itself a wonder and a glory, the crowning of his career as an artist. But more wonderful and

glorious still would be the moment in which
he was to set it before the eyes of its model.

In what possible way could he more fully
and thoroughly make the girl his own than by
capturing, fastening and fixing upon his canvas
every line and hue of her young body, her complete, carefully hidden beauty, going over it,
patting and dubbing every item of it with his
brush, re-creating and immortalizing it, so that
nobody in the world could ever again separate
the two of them. It would be, unmistakably and
for all eternity, Ehrengard, the maid from the
mountains, and it would be, unmistakably and
for all eternity, a Cazotte.

In the picture the face of the bather would
be turned away. By no means would he betray
or give away his maid-of-honor. He might show
his masterpiece to Princes and Princesses, art
critics and enraptured lay lookers-on, and to
the girl herself at the same moment, and no one
but he and she would know the truth. The con-
noisseurs round her would break out in delight
at the beauty of the bathing figure; in little ex-

pert remarks they would, with their thumbs in the air, minutely go through this latest and loveliest nude of that great painter Cazotte. She would be, in the midst of the brilliant crowd, alone with him.

Her mind never worked quickly, it would take her two or three minutes to grasp her position. Three facts she would at the end of them have made her own. That she was beautiful. That she was naked—and already in the third chapter of Genesis such a recognition is reported to be fatal. And, lastly, that in being thus beautiful and naked she had given herself over to the Venusberg. And to him.

The figure on the canvas would remain chastely silvery before the ardent eyes of the spectators. But the maiden by his side would slowly become all aglow. Behind the shawl, silk gown, embroidered petticoats and dainty cambric, the straight, strong, pure body from heel to forehead would blush into a deep exquisite crimson, a mystical *rose persan*, which no clear water of a mountain lake would ever wash away.

Into that Alpen-Glühen upon which night follows!

No one in the world, and least of all she
herself, would ever find words for the relation
between her and him. But from that moment
whenever he bid her farewell, he would be
abandoning and forsaking her.

Herr Cazotte drew a deep sigh.

But indeed, indeed, he went on after a
while, the Gods are dangerous playfellows, and
he would have to be wary and watchful to the
utmost degree. He must lie in wait, dead still,
like the lion waiting for the antelope by the
water hole. The faintest movement might ruin
him forever. For had not, from the very beginning, he himself, the artist and arbiter, the true
lover and servant of this young womanhood
decreed that she were to blush not with indignation at an assault, but with ecstasy at a
revelation, not in protest or self-defense, but in
consent and surrender!

Herr Cazotte was of small assistance to
Princess Ludmilla in the arrangement of her pro-

gram. All through the evening he was so silent that in the end Prince Lothar laughingly cried to him: "Wolfgang, you are planning a new picture!" The painter looked up, grew a little pale, and after a moment very gravely answered: "Yes, forgive me. But I have got an order for a new picture."

The next day he travelled to Babenhausen in order to buy canvas, brushes and paint. And the following morning found him among the bush of the bank, setting up his easel and stretcher, and then waiting patiently for sunrise and for the vision of three days ago. The sunlight was on the higher slopes of the mountains and on the treetops when once more he caught the low, gentle women's voices approaching. The scene was the same as the first morning, and the whole of Herr Cazotte was in his firm hand as he put down his primary contours on the canvas.

Time was short, all too short, in a quarter of an hour she was gone. The sun shone on the lake and the landscape, but their soul had left them, leaving him himself in a vacuum as if he had suddenly gone blind. He took down his easel and collected his drawing things. He would have, every morning, this divine *quart d'heure*. For the rest of the day he kept the vision behind eyes closed to everything else. He locked the door to his study and kept the key in his pocket.

He worked on for a week, radiating a new mystic happiness, but silent, humble in mien and manner and particularly humble and submissive towards Ehrengard when the two were brought together by the daily life of the chateau. Only every morning he had a heart-rending moment when his nymph went away.

Then on the last day of the week her disappearance seemed to him more sudden than before, indeed inexplicably sudden. A sigh or a short subdued outcry, which could not have come from Ehrengard but might have been the maid's, went through the morning landscape— then it was like watching a doe in a wood: she was there, and then she was there no more, the space was empty.

He needed more tubes of paint and again went to Babenhausen. There in the colorshop he was struck by an instantaneous deadly apprehension. Ehrengard or her maid, he thought, might have spied him in the morning, and that might have been the reason for their supernatural disappearance. He dismissed the idea, he knew from experience that sooner or later in the course of a piece of work he would be the victim of some such terrible nervous misgiving. But he could not free himself of it, and on his return journey was both longing for and dreading his next meeting with Ehrengard. Would her face tell him without a word that there was to be no more bathing of Diana and that the glory of his life was never to be achieved?

He came back to Rosenbad late in the afternoon and found the ladies of the court assembled in the Princess' pale blue boudoir, which was filled like an aviary with twitter and trills of laughter.

During this last week the court had been curiously moved and agitated. For at the end of it the little Prince was to make his legal and ceremonial entry in the world. On Saturday the goal would be reached, the danger would be over, and therefore everybody was gay. But on Saturday, too, a strange, a dreamlike period would come to an end, the child would no longer be the secret of Rosenbad, and therefore everybody was a little sad.

The Princess today was *coiffée* for the first time and dressed in a pretty white negligée. She had watched the nurse bathing the baby, had snatched him from her aproned lap, and insisted on carrying him into her own room, still all shining like a figurine in the midst of a fountain. She was now, on the sofa, gently rolling him about on her knees and rubbing him in the lace of her peignoir. The Oberhofmeisterin, in an armchair by the sofa, repeatedly assured the mother that the child was really smiling. Ehrengard was standing up looking at the baby.

"O my dear friend," the Princess cried out at the sight of the painter, "you have come at the right moment. I feel, I am convinced, that never again, not even tomorrow, will he be as adorable as he is this afternoon. Do catch this perfect moment . . ."

"This momentary perfection," put in Countess Poggendorff.

". . . Pin it to your canvas and preserve it for the world to adore."

The child had grown lovelier with each of his sixty days, his small body was firm, smooth and dimpled, and as light as if he might at any moment lift himself and fly off. He was an easy and amiable baby and was seldom heard to cry. Herr Cazotte from time to time had been drawing up in charcoal and pastel small portraits of him, the which in due time, in September, would be shown in the Babenhausen gallery as illustrations of the infant's progress.

"Look at him, dear good Herr Cazotte," the Princess exclaimed. "Surely you will be needing a model for an amorino in a scene of love. I lend him to you for the purpose."

The gardener had just brought up a very large flat basket filled with fresh, abundant white stocks, and the lackey had placed it on the floor.

"Hand me the basket, sweetest Poggendorff," said Ludmilla. "I am sure that it is exactly like the basket in which the Princess of

Egypt found little Moses amongst the rushes. Poor, poor Princess, how she must have wept at the thought that he was not her own."

As the Oberhofmeisterin lifted up the basket, the Princess placed the baby upon the fragrant couch. "You have not looked at him nearly enough," she cried to Herr Cazotte. "Take the basket, Ehrengard, and hold it up for the Master to inspect."

At her request Ehrengard lifted the basket and the child from the Princess' knee, and on her strong arms presented them to Herr Cazotte. The painter, still reluctant to look her in the face, let his eyes rest on the baby. But the pose of her figure recalled to him a group by the great sculptor Thorvaldsen, "Psyche selling amorini." For a minute he stood quite still, his face like hers bowed over the fairy cradle. The scent of the stocks, an invisible cloud of Venusberg incense, encompassed their two heads. She was calm and happy, he felt; he might be calm and happy with her, with full confidence in the Gods.

"Princess," he said, "you have given me a

more than princely gift. For as the hart panteth after the water brook, so panteth the soul of the artist after his motif. And who knows whether the motif does not long for that work of art in which it is to be made its true self."

Lispeth appeared in the doorway, anxious about the unorthodox treatment of the baby. The little Prince was lifted from his bed of flowers, given back to the arms of his nurse, where he immediately began to squall, and carried away. Ludmilla drew Ehrengard down to her side on the sofa and put her arm round her waist.

"O Ehrengard," she said. "How I do wish that Prince Lothar and I had been even more thoughtless than we have, and that we had got a month more at Rosenbad."

The evening of that day was the most glorious of the summer. A golden light filled the air as golden wine fills a glass.

The Princess went to bed early. The Oberhofmeisterin, the maid-of-honor and the court painter made their usual tour of the garden. But Countess Poggendorff began to feel

the air a little cool and was the first to return to
the house, the two younger people following her
slowly on the gravel path. Herr Cazotte wondered whether Ehrengard, as upon an earlier
evening, was thinking of nothing at all.

As upon that earlier evening they passed
the Leda fountain. Ehrengard slowed her steps,
stopped and stood for a moment with the tips of
her fingers in the clear water of the basin from
which the breast and the proud neck of the swan
rose towards Leda's knees. As she lifted her
head, turned and faced Herr Cazotte, she was a
little pale, but she spoke in a clear voice.

"My maid tells me," she said, "that you
want to paint a picture. Out by the east of the
house. I wish to tell you that I shall be there
every morning, at six o'clock."

Herr Cazotte wrote:

My dear good Friend,
The damnable, the dynamic, the de-
monic loyalty of this girl!
Yours in fear and trembling,
Cazotte

Here, said the old lady who told the story, finishes that second part of my story which I have named "Rosenbad." It has gone a little slowly, I know—so, generally speaking, do pastorales. Now, to make up for the lost time, the last movement of my small sonata shall be a rondo, which perhaps you may even find to end up *con furore.*

❧

It has been told in the beginning of this tale that there existed in the Grand Duchy of Babenhausen a lateral branch to the dynasty. These fine people with their head, the Duke Marbod, a gentleman who had spent most of his life out of his own country and had married a lady-in-waiting to the Queen of Naples, we have been able to leave for a while to themselves, since they had been lying low from the time of Prince Lothar's wedding. Some of them had even shaken the dust of Babenhausen off their feet and taken up their residence elsewhere. Now unfortunately they come back into the

tale as they came back into the country, sneak-
ing upon a track and drawn by a scent.

For there is a strange quality about a secret:
it smells of secrecy. You may be far from getting the true nature of the secret itself, you
might even, had it been told you, be highly skep-
tical and incredulous of it—yet you will feel
certain that a secret there be.

The early misgivings of the Grand Duch-
ess in regard to the all too celestial nature of her
son had been vague and undefined, she lacked
knowledge of the world and of the nature of
man to put them into words. Duke Marbod and
his friends, who were of a grosser fabric, had
had no scruples in setting up on their own a
definite hypothesis of the case. Something about
the Rosenbad establishment and the complete
seclusion of the Princess and her court, set a
cantankerous imagination running, and in the
end a highly fantastic story circulating in the
gang. Young Prince Lothar, it was declared,
was incapable of being the father of a child, and
Princess Ludmilla's pregnancy was all a farce.
The ruling house, foreseeing its doom, was

quietly preparing to hoodwink the nation, to carry through the pretence and in the end, in order to keep their rivals out of their rights, to present to a loyal people a child of obscure origin as heir to the throne. Absurd and unseemly rumors about pads provided for the transformation of the Young Princess' slim figure were made up—enough of that. The pack, as we ourselves will know, was running on a wrong scent; all the same, as we will also know, it was running on a scent.

Duke Marbod himself, who was never a man of many ideas, at the utmost reflected that it may always pay to fish in troubled water. But his partisans let their ideas multiply. In the end two of them, one a former officer of the hussars, the other a man about town, a wine merchant, took up their abode in "The Blue Boar," the inn of a village some five miles from Schloss Rosenbad, awaiting a chance to pry into the stronghold.

A very small and poor fish caught in their net was mistress Lispeth's husband, a young peasant named Matthias. This boy by his father-

in-law, the gamekeeper, had been suspected of
poaching and had long held a grudge against the
whole of his wife's family. Now he felt himself
ill-used beyond endurance by being robbed of
his pretty wife. The mother of a suckling baby
and of two children only a few years older had
been tempted away from her home in order to
act as chambermaid to a spoilt great young lady,
who must needs have all her whims attended to,
for, as his wife had definitely informed him,
there was no baby to nurse at Rosenbad. The
thing went against his peasant's sense of decency,
it was as if you would have a fine milk cow cart
flowers to market. On top of all he was from
the very beginning jealous of Prince Lothar's
valet.

Matthias had come up from his farm a
couple of times and had been allowed into the
lodge of the chateau to see his wife and give her
news of the children. But his querulousness and
jealousy on these visits had upset Lispeth, after
each of them the little Prince had yelled his
protest, and Professor Putziger had had to put
an end to the meetings. Still the unhappy young

husband would or could not go home, but came prowling round the forbidden area.

On the morning of the fourteenth of July he waylaid his wife as she was taking the air in the park and through the lattice of the gate told her that, convinced of her treacherousness, he would kill the valet or himself. Lispeth did not take his threats seriously, but she was terrified of a scandal at this moment and could see no other way out of the dilemma than to disclose part of the truth to her husband. Yes, there was a baby at Rosenbad. She could at the moment give him no further information, he must take it for what it was and might come to understand in time. If he would solemnly swear to her that he would go home immediately after, she would bring down the child to the gate in the afternoon, so that he could see it with his own eyes. Matthias took the oath, walked back to a small inn quite close to the chateau where he had left his mare and cart, and there to clear his confused mind emptied a bottle of wine. It was at this moment that he fell into the hands of Duke Marbod's intriguers.

The two gentlemen by this time had almost given up the hunt. They had not been able to get into touch with the Rosenbad household, only at a distance had they seen Prince Lothar, Herr Cazotte and Ehrengard riding by, and Herr Cazotte had been right inasmuch as that the presence of the young maid-of-honor averted suspicions of double dealing. They were about to return somewhat crestfallen to Duke Marbod, but had come up close to the gates for a last attempt. By chance they got into conversation with Matthias, who over his bottle babbled out the list of his misfortunes, his wife's shamelessness and the villainy of the whole court in barring out her lawful husband.

The gentlemen looked at one another.

In the eleventh hour they found themselves to have been right. Surprisingly, mysteriously, their own fancies and fabrications took shape before their eyes, and proof was at hand. After a short consultation, while pouring more wine into their informant, they gravely initiated him into the situation: a dangerous plot was in progress at the Schloss. They could at the moment give him no further information. But it was a matter of high treason, and very likely, as he had been suggesting, Prince Lothar's valet was at the head of it.

This much they could promise him, that in case he could manage to carry off the woman and the child and deliver them into their hands at "The Blue Boar," he would be rendering a great service to his country, and they would pay him out on the spot a reward of a hundred thaler. Matthias was not so much moved by these prospects as by the satisfaction of long-wanted sympathy, also in seeing his personal grievances exalted into an affair of state he got back some of his self-confidence.

Thus it happened that in the afternoon of the fourteenth of July the husband brought his cart to the gate of the park, was shown the child, and told his wife that he did now believe in her innocence and was ready to forget all. As the two were taking a final leave, he managed to lure the unsuspecting woman outside the gate and even to make her put her foot on the nave of the wheel and lift up the child in order

that he might kiss it. At that moment he seized
her round the waist with one arm and dragged
her onto the seat of his cart, while with his other
arm he slashed the mare wildly with the reins
and made her start into a mad gallop. Lispeth
gave one long, terrible scream. But a minute
later they were at the foot of the hill in a thick
cloud of dust, and once out of earshot from the
chateau and the park the unhappy woman dared
not cry for help. She clung to the child and the
seat and burst into a storm of tears.

During the whole mad drive of almost an
hour no word was exchanged between the ab-
ductor and the victim, and no argument put
forth from either side. It would indeed have
been difficult to catch any word spoken in the
rumble and clatter which surrounded and followed the cart like a thick swarm of angry bees,
or to think of any argument while the small
vehicle was being flung up and down and from
right to left on rough, stony roads. All the same
husband and wife, pressed together, were in
some way communicating and acting upon one
another.

Lispeth had at once realized with deadly clearness that she was hopelessly in the power of the blunt, silent figure beside her. He had outwitted, lost and ruined her, and with her the Princess and the whole circle of people who had put their trust in her. She had thought him a fool, and he was a fool, but he was something else and worse, he had in him a dreadful cruelty which she had never suspected. She wept loudly and without restraint.

Matthias, who had vowed that no protest on his wife's part should move his heart, in the course of the drive was slowly being converted and brought into a state of contrition by that fine thing: the righteous fury of an honest person. Vaguely he felt the distance between the countrywoman in his cart, smelling from clean starched linen and bathed in artless tears, and the new urbane plotting friends smelling from pomade, waiting for him in the inn, and of the monstrousness of delivering the former into the hands of the latter. But tossed from side to side both bodily and spiritually he was incapable of forming any plan, and after a while left matters in charge of his mare.

This patient animal, possibly the most indignant of the group, could not go on forever at her first mad rate; as her master lost heart she slowed down. Lispeth then sat up a little, drew a deep breath and looked round.

Through the mist of her tears and the beginning dusk she saw a great many mounted soldiers galloping in the fields to all sides of her. She remembered the big maneuvers going on and somehow took courage, soldiers in uniform were decent people and would side with a woman against a madman and murderer. A short time later the road ran through a village and up to an inn which the mare knew, she stopped before its door. Matthias gave in to her, pushed his cap back on his head and silently, almost humbly, climbed down and helped his wife and the child to the ground. Dusk was coming on, there were lights in the windows of "The Blue Boar."

Behind them there was both high glee and merriment, and deep anxiousness.

The maneuvers were over. The officers were celebrating the occasion by a dinner in the big common room, from which loud talk and laughter rang. Here Kurt von Blittersdorff, who had distinguished himself in a cavalry attack, was being congratulated by his colonel. In a smaller room behind the hall there was silence. Duke Marbod's followers had not been prepared for the big gay gathering, they were afraid of being recognized and questioned, had chosen to lie low, and sat without words on two chairs, at times looking at one another.

Lispeth, Matthias and the child, like a second Holy Family of mystical inside relationship, were met at the door with the information that there was no room for them in the inn. Lispeth, sore-limbed and swaying on her feet with exhaustion, had only one thought: to find a place where she could feed the baby, and no words to express her need. But a kind of desperate determination in her mien and carriage, like that of a soldier dying on his post, moved the heart of a little maid of the inn, who herself had got young brothers and sisters at home, and who obtained for her a small room upstairs, where she could at last sink down on a chair and unbutton her bodice. The moment she had laid the child to the breast both became perfectly calm.

Matthias meanwhile slunk away to unharness the mare in the stable of the inn, highly nervous that his employers should somehow appear, or send for him, and happy when inexplicably they did not. He told the people of the inn that he had got nothing to do with anybody there and was going to leave as soon as his wife had had a rest. He then again slunk upstairs and sat down on a stool with his back to the wall in the exact manner of his friends down below. The little maid after a while brought up a candle and a tray with milk and bread and remnants from the officers' table.

During the time when these things were happening on the road and in the inn, emotions of a no less volcanic nature filled the rooms behind the silk curtains of Schloss Rosenbad.

When the child and his nurse were found missing, enquiries, at first only slightly uneasy, then inspired by growing fear and in the end by horror and dismay, were made in all directions. The baby and the nurse, it was said, had last been seen in the park. But a gardener's boy reported that he had observed Lispeth talking to a man outside the gate, and soon it was known that a cart with a man and a woman in it had been tearing down the road at incredible speed. There was no mistaking the fact that the little Prince had been kidnapped.

How, now, was Rosenbad to take in the truth and survive it? The cannons of the citadel of Babenhausen were held ready to proclaim, on the very next day, the birth of an heir to the throne, the flags of the palace were laid forth to be hoisted and fill the air over the towers with gay colors. Was the roar of triumph to be quelled in those iron throats and the sky to be left empty? Had the incessant watch of two months been in vain, and was the glory of Babenhausen to prove still-born? And oh, the child, the child—the trusting, laughing baby, the apple of the eye of Rosenbad—was he to be flung all alone into a hard world, possibly never to be seen again?

Two months ago when the very small voice had first been heard in its rooms, the house had been lifted off the ground to float, a temple of happiness, in the air above the lake and the green slopes. Now within one short hour it was overthrown as by an earthquake and was left roofless, open to all the winds of heaven, a ruin.

At first neither of the unhappy parents was informed of their misfortune. Prince Lothar had gone to town to bring his mother Herr Cazotte's latest miniature of the baby and would not be back till evening. Princess Ludmilla was studying the texts of her Italian songs for the concert and had given instructions that she was not to be disturbed.

But Countess Poggendorff in the garden room actually fell on her knees with the weight of all the falling stones of the chateau upon her delicate shoulders. When she got some of her strength back she rang the bell and sent for Herr Cazotte, and when he appeared she threw herself into his arms.

This heart-rending news, she declared in a faint and broken voice, must by all means be kept from the Princess, who might take her death from it, and meanwhile rescuers would have to be sent out to all four corners of the earth. But O my dear Herr Cazotte, who was wise and discreet enough to be trusted with a mission so momentous and so delicate!

Herr Cazotte at once ordered his small gig made ready and his cloak and hat brought down. While he waited he stood silent, with a thoughtful face.

As usual, he knew more than other people. He had seen Matthias on one of the man's vain expeditions to the chateau, he had even talked with him and had some of the offended husband's grudges confided to him. On one of his trips to town, upon a hot day, he had stopped at "The Blue Boar" to have a drink, and there had met the two conspirators, who were old acquaintances of his. He now put two and two together and blamed himself for having been so absorbed in a single work of art as to overlook the artifice of baser minds in the neighborhood.

But the terrible news was not unwelcome to him. After his last walk by the Leda fountain with Ehrengard he had passed a bad night and had left his work untouched in the morning. Now he saw that although they had been playing him a trick, those dangerous playfellows of his, the Gods, were with him still. The course of things was inspiring, and of all things in the world Herr Cazotte really with his whole heart wanted only one: inspiration. From the present situation almost any other might arise, and Herr Cazotte was a collector and connoisseur of situations.

The first of these presented itself when Ehrengard came into the room, in her riding habit and just back from her ride, and Madame Poggendorff turned from Herr Cazotte to fall on the neck of the girl, sobbing as unrestrainedly as an hour before had Lispeth in the cart and on the road. As soon as she was enlightened upon the catastrophe Ehrengard again pulled on her riding gloves to go in pursuit of

the criminals. Countess Poggendorff begged
her to go with Herr Cazotte in his gig, she did
not like the thought of her facing these scoun-
drels all alone, and it was getting late. No, said
Ehrengard, she was not afraid. Wotan was quite
fresh, she had been out exercising Prince
Lothar's mount for him, and she would be
quicker on horseback than in a carriage. She
knew all the roads and paths in the neighborhood, and if she were to stay out late she was
used to riding at night.

Herr Cazotte did not try to hold her back.
If she had the advantage of getting off before
him, he on his side had a surer track to go upon.
During the minutes in which he stood watching
the tearful older and the flaming younger
woman, a succession of charming pictures passed
through his mind. He would be presenting the
regained child to the girl to give back into its
mother's arms, he might even be on his knees before her to do so. An amorino, the Princess had
called her baby, an amorino indeed, joining, as
with a garland of roses, a human couple. Would
the girl not feel then for a vertiginous moment

this particular amorino to be, spiritually and emotionally, her own child—and his! He himself got her into the saddle.

Wotan was in high spirits, when Ehrengard reined him in to question people on the road he reared, and she was so filled with indignation against the kidnappers on whose track she was trotting that she beat her mount with her riding whip. All the same she was happy, it was as if for a long time she had yearned to be angry. She was Ehrengard, no one could take that away from her, and, strangely, it was a privilege. The evening air was getting cooler, she rode through many spheres of fragrance: clover, flowering lime trees, and drying strawberry fields, through them all the ammoniac smell of the lathering horse was the strongest. She drew in her breath deeply, and ran on, with raised head and distended nostrils, a young female centaur playing along the grass fields.

She had the hunting instincts of her breed, it was not difficult to her to run the fugitives to earth in "The Blue Boar." The cart was still standing outside the stable, and she learned from an ostler of the inn that the man, the woman and the child were in the house, possibly, she thought, behind the lighted window above her head. She left Wotan in the man's care, ordering him to walk him up and down for half an hour and then to rub him well with a wisp of straw. There were, she noticed, a number of soldiers about the place, she felt happier still at this sight, they were people of her own kind, and it was as if she had got home.

Up in the small room behind the lighted window a temporary peace ruled. Lispeth had fallen into a short slumber with the child still at her breast. But Matthias was wide awake on his stool with his back to the wall. For a long hour he had been trying hard to sound the depth of his misfortune, from time to time also wondering what his fellow conspirators were doing, or thinking of him. The presence of his wife, however, the familiar sight of her suckling a baby and the familiar feeling that she would be able, somehow, to put things right, in the end had quieted his nerves. When she woke up, he reflected, he would drive her straight back to

Rosenbad. And possibly all might still be well.

He was startled out of this state of hope when the door was flung open and Ehrengard stood on the threshold. The girl in the ride had lost her hat, her long fair hair streamed down and framed her face and figure, to the guilty man those of a young destroying angel.

Lispeth, waking up too, saw the girl in the same light, but conscious of her innocence she at once welcomed the angel of revenge in a glance as expressive as an outcry. She remained perfectly still on her chair, only in a hardly perceptible movement of her arm she raised the baby's head so as to show that he was unhurt.

Ehrengard's gaze responded to Lispeth's in a declaration of perfect trust, then she turned to the kidnapper. The inviolable obligation of silence controlled the girl as well as the woman, she said not a word. But here, at the final goal of her ride, the old feudal consciousness of the right to punish seized and held the daughter of the Schreckensteins. She would have died rather than have foregone her office of chastiser.

She had left her riding whip with the horse

and was barehanded for the execution, she gripped Matthias by his long hair and three times knocked his head against the wall behind him till the room darkened and swam before his eyes. He gave out a row of low wails which, however, far from frightening his tormentor, infuriated her into striking him in the face with her fist, so that the blood spouted from his nose. In actual fear of his life, of being knocked to pieces by the strong young hands that held him, he made his cries for help ring through the house.

Down at the officers' dinner table the talk happened to have turned upon ghosts. One of the party had been recounting an old tale of "The Blue Boar" itself. A hundred years ago a jealous husband had followed his runaway wife and her lover to the inn, had found them together in a room upstairs and had dealt the seducer the treatment of Abelard. At certain times at night the gruesome scene was repeated in the room. At this moment Matthias let out his screams.

These were indeed pitiful enough to have moved the hearts of the dinner party, who probably feared the lot of the victim in the tale more than anything else in life. At the same time they were so far from being connected with any idea of romance that the short alarmed silence round the table was immediately swallowed up in laughter.

"You go up, Kurt," the colonel cried to that young officer, "and find out if it be ghosts or people. And come back whole yourself."

The tall young man pushed back his chair and left the room, followed by various loud and gay remarks. As he ran up the stairs, the screams from above were repeated.

He opened a door, and in a dimly lit small room caught sight of a deadly pale man pressed up against the wall by a slender young woman in a riding coat with long waves of golden hair flowing down her back. From a chair by the window a woman with a baby on her lap, with wide-open eyes but without a word, watched the scene.

When she heard the door open behind her, the Amazon let go her hold of the man and turned round.

"Ehrengard!" Kurt von Blittersdorff cried out in the highest amazement.

The girl's cheeks as she tossed back her hair were all aflame and her eyes shining. She opened her lips as if to cry his own name back, then stiffened, like a child caught red-handed.

The whole absurd situation was so much like one of their childhood romps that the young man almost burst out laughing. At the same time he felt uneasy about the girl's presence in the inn, with his fellow officers waiting for him downstairs.

"Ehrengard! What on earth are you doing here?" he asked.

The released sufferer profited by the respite to wriggle himself out of reach of his assaulter. He fumblingly ran his fingers through his hair, making it stand up straight like the quills of a hedgehog, and whimpered a couple of times. Although he was at the moment safe from molestation, he realized his position to be graver than before. Here was a gentleman, an officer, obviously a friend of his enemy and welcomed by her, unexpectedly on the stage. With three judges upon him what hope had he? Still, as a silence followed on the officer's exclamation he blindly groped for a way out and started on a harangue of defense.

"So God help me, Sir," he said, "I am a perfectly innocent man, and this is a very unfair attack on the part of the lady. That," he went on, pointing at the woman with the baby, "is my lawful wife. You ask her yourself, Sir, she will not deny it. Has the lady, has the lodge-keeper, has the Prince's valet, or has he himself, then, got any right to keep her away from me? They have not, Sir, and they know so themselves. For what God has joined together," he cried in a stroke of inspiration, "let man not put asunder."

He stopped for a moment, but his nerves could not bear the continued silence of the others in the room.

"So God help me, Sir," he started again, "it is I who am wronged. I want my lawful wife back, that is all I want. She tells me she cannot leave the child. Well, then let her take the child

with her. I have not tried to stop her from taking
the child with her. Only ask her if I have done
so."

The lasting silence, Ehrengard's fury a little
while ago, his wife's despair in the cart, and the
persuasion and promise of the two gentlemen
from town, if Matthias had been able to see these
things as a whole, by now might have made the
entire pattern dawn upon him. It was not so, his
sore head reeled, anything might have thrown
him in any direction. But hares, when the
hounds are after them, in their wildest side leaps
will show a kind of genius. Something in the atmosphere of the room suddenly told him where
his chance of escape lay. It was with the child.

The child, who after the strenuous journey
was now firmly asleep on Lispeth's bosom, was
the mystery which his wife and the angry lady
did by no means want solved. If he let out that
he could do so if he wished, they might think
more highly of him, they might even consent to
buy his silence. As he spoke on he felt that he
was on the right track.

"My wife, Sir," he said, "will tell you that

I have got no claim on the child, for it is not mine. If that is what the lady is going to tell you as well, let them tell you whose child it is."

Kurt gave Lispeth a short glance, then looked back at Ehrengard. Both women seemed to have been struck dumb by the man's speech. The situation, till now merely inexplicable, began to take on a different, a more momentous aspect. He must, he felt, put an end to a scene obviously beneath the dignity of his fiancée.

"Come," he said, "you cannot stay here. What have you got to do with these peasants? Why do you not leave them to settle their quarrels between themselves? I shall arrange at once for some convenience to take you back to Rosenbad."

He had not succeeded in getting one word out of her, neither did he do so now.

"There you see, Sir," cried Matthias triumphantly. "Neither of them will tell you."

There was a short pause.

"Well," Kurt asked in a steady voice. "Do tell me, Ehrengard. What child is it?"

At this moment they heard light steps coming up the stairs. It was Herr Cazotte who had arrived in his gig and who now entered the room.

He took in the situation in one glance. But he felt that at the moment and under the circumstances it did not fall to him to interfere. He placed his hat on the bed and after a minute sat down on the bed himself. There he remained, like some highly intelligent looker-on in a *fauteuil d'orchestre*, keenly interested in the drama on the stage and in full understanding with the fact that none of the *dramatis personae* took any interest whatever in him himself.

"You see, Sir," Matthias repeated in the same way. "They will not even answer you, neither of them."

Kurt, moved by a new strange, deep concern, again followed Matthias' lead.

"What child is it?" he asked.

Ehrengard still met his eyes and still did not answer.

"But if you will not answer me," Kurt said lowly, "I cannot help this woman or interfere with her husband."

She stood up straight, as if pondering his words.

"If you will not answer me," he said, "How am I to understand that you be here at all?"

Ehrengard said: "It is my child."

The young man had drunk a good deal during dinner, but up in this room he had believed the effect of the wine to have left him. Now at her declaration his head failed him, he must, he realized, have drunk more than he had been aware of. He laughed.

"Say that again," he cried. But as he would by no means have her say it again he went on: "Are you all mad up here? Come away with me."

"I shall say it again," said Ehrengard, and after a moment: "It is my child.

"You may ask Lispeth," she went on, "she will bear me up. This man, who is really, as he tells you, her husband, has kidnapped both the child and his nurse. I have gone after them and have found them here."

There was a long pause.

"It will," said Ehrengard, "as you say, be the best thing to get a carriage and go back. It is good of you to offer to help me. But I cannot accept your help unless you will give me your word that when you have brought me back to Rosenbad you will leave me forever."

Slowly and solemnly she once more announced, "For it is my child."

Kurt had grown very pale, his mind ran wildly through the time in which he had not seen her. His instinct of self-preservation cried out to him that she had gone mad. Again he laughed, a short pathetic laugh. But he could not go on laughing in front of her deadly earnest face, in a little while he became as grave as she.

"You will have to believe me," Ehrengard said. "I have never in my life lied to you."

He stood on looking at her. There had been, he now saw, a change in her since their last meeting six months ago. With the candle behind her and her mass of hair hanging down, she seemed to float in a mist of gold, much lovelier than he had ever seen her, much lovelier than any woman he had ever seen, a goddess or a demon. How was it that he had known her so long, had played with her, ridden with her, wrestled with her, had known that some day he was to marry her, and that until this hour he had not known that she was the most lovely thing on earth, and the one thing necessary to his happiness? This state of mind of his lasted for about a minute, then he knew for certain that he had always known.

It took him some time to form an answer. His faith in her, of so many years, together with his new need of her, contracted his throat and made it impossible for him to get out his voice.

"You will help me, then," said she, "and take me home. Then we must part. You must never speak of me. You must never think of me."

To Ehrengard, too, something was happening as here she stood up straight, face to face with Kurt's straight figure. She too felt, in a new way, the depth of life. There was a sweetness in it which till now she had never known of, there was a terrible sadness as well. She would never have believed, had anybody told her, that to meet and to part with Kurt von Blittersdorff could mean so much. The recognition at this moment was, she felt, the outcome of her stay at Rosenbad.

"Yes," Kurt said at last. "I shall do as you ask me. I shall go now and get the carriage to drive you back. I shall then leave you forever. I shall not speak of you more than I absolutely need. I shall try, as you say, not to think of you."

There was another pause.

"But," he went on slowly and lowly, "there is one question to which I must have an answer from you. I have no right to ask you. But neither have you any right to ask me never to think of you again. And that cannot be done, I cannot possibly leave off thinking of you, unless you answer it. Who is the father of the child?"

A silence. Neither the young man nor the girl could have told whether it lasted for a minute or an hour. The other people in the room sank through the floor, he and she were alone as on a mountain peak.

"It will be, Ehrengard," he said, "a secret between you and me, a thing which, in the whole world, only you and I know of."

Ehrengard had grown as pale as he. So colorless did her face become that her light eyes seemed dark in it, like two cavities. Then she turned and looked straight at Herr Cazotte. Under her glance the gentleman rose from the bed.

The girl's glance was strong and direct, like an arrow's course from the bowstring to the target. In it she flung her past, present and future at his feet.

She lifted her arm, like a young officer at his baptism of fire indicating to his men the entrenchment to be taken, and pointed at him.

"It is he," she said. "Herr Cazotte is the father of my child."

At these words Herr Cazotte's blood was drawn upwards, as from the profoundest wells of his being, till it colored him all over like a transparent crimson veil. His brow and cheeks, all on their own, radiated a divine fire, a celestial, deep rose flame, as if they were giving away a long kept secret.

And it was a strange thing that he should blush. For normally an onlooker in a *fauteuil d'orchestre* would grow pale at seeing the irate hero of the stage suddenly turn upon him. The actual situation held very grave possibilities to Herr Cazotte. A duel might be the immediate consequence of it, and Herr Cazotte, as it is known, disliked the sight of human blood outside the human body. Any gallant warrior of Babenhausen, knowing Kurt von Blittersdorff's reputation with a sword or a pistol, might have gone white, even white as death.

But Herr Cazotte, who was an artist, blushed.

Here ends the story of Ehrengard.

❧

But as I gave you a prelude to my story, said the old lady who told it, I shall give you an epilogue.

No duel took place. By the mediation of Prince Lothar and Princess Ludmilla a full understanding was obtained. A week later the betrothed couple Kurt and Ehrengard were present at the baptism of the new-born Prince in the Dom of Babenhausen.

Upon this occasion the girl wore, across the bodice of her white satin frock, the light blue ribbon of the Order of St. Stephan, the which is a distinction given to noble ladies for merits in the service of the house of Fugger-Babenhausen.

Herr Cazotte to the surprise of the court was not present at the ceremony. He had been called back to Rome to paint a portrait of the Pope.

It was here, now, that he had that famous liaison with a *cantatrice* of the Opera which caused much talk and made his acquaintances smilingly alter his name to that of Casanova.

When the Grand Duchess heard of it she was upset.

"I had really," she said, "during that time at Rosenbad, come to have such faith in Geheim-rat Cazotte."

MORE ABOUT PENGUINS, PELICANS
AND PUFFINS

For further information about books available from Penguins please write to Dept EP, Penguin Books Ltd, Harmondsworth, Middlesex UB7 0DA.

In the U.S.A.: For a complete list of books available from Penguins in the United States write to Dept DG, Penguin Books, 299 Murray Hill Parkway, East Rutherford, New Jersey 07073.

In Canada: For a complete list of books available from Penguins in Canada write to Penguin Books Canada Limited, 2801 John Street, Markham, Ontario L3R 1B4.

In Australia: For a complete list of books available from Penguins in Australia write to the Marketing Department, Penguin Books Australia Ltd, P.O. Box 257, Ringwood, Victoria 3134.

In New Zealand: For a complete list of books available from Penguins in New Zealand write to the Marketing Department, Penguin Books (N.Z.) Ltd, Private Bag, Takapuna, Auckland 9.

In India: For a complete list of books available from Penguins in India write to Penguin Overseas Ltd, 706 Eros Apartments, 56 Nehru Place, New Delhi 110019.

A CHOICE OF PENGUINS

☐ **Small World** **David Lodge**   £2.50

A jet-propelled academic romance, sequel to *Changing Places*. 'A new comic débâcle on every page' – *The Times*. 'Here is everything one expects from Lodge but three times as entertaining as anything he has written before' – *Sunday Telegraph*

☐ **The Neverending Story** **Michael Ende**   £3.95

The international bestseller, now a major film: 'A tale of magical adventure, pursuit and delay, danger, suspense, triumph' – *The Times Literary Supplement*

☐ **The Sword of Honour Trilogy** **Evelyn Waugh**   £3.95

Containing *Men at Arms, Officers and Gentlemen* and *Unconditional Surrender*, the trilogy described by Cyril Connolly as 'unquestionably the finest novels to have come out of the war'.

☐ **The Honorary Consul** **Graham Greene**   £2.50

In a provincial Argentinian town, a group of revolutionaries kidnap the wrong man . . . 'The tension never relaxes and one reads hungrily from page to page, dreading the moment it will all end' – Auberon Waugh in the *Evening Standard*

☐ **The First Rumpole Omnibus** **John Mortimer**   £4.95

Containing *Rumpole of the Bailey, The Trials of Rumpole* and *Rumpole's Return*. 'A fruity, foxy masterpiece, defender of our wilting faith in mankind' – *Sunday Times*

☐ **Scandal** **A. N. Wilson**   £2.25

Sexual peccadillos, treason and blackmail are all ingredients on the boil in A. N. Wilson's new, *cordon noir* comedy. 'Drily witty, deliciously nasty' – *Sunday Telegraph*

A CHOICE OF PENGUINS

☐ *Stanley and the Women* **Kingsley Amis** £2.50

'Very good, very powerful . . . beautifully written . . . This is Amis
père at his best' – Anthony Burgess in the *Observer*. 'Everybody
should read it' – *Daily Mail*

☐ *The Mysterious Mr Ripley* **Patricia Highsmith** £4.95

Containing *The Talented Mr Ripley, Ripley Underground* and
Ripley's Game. 'Patricia Highsmith is the poet of apprehension' –
Graham Greene. 'The Ripley books are marvellously, insanely read-
able' – *The Times*

☐ *Earthly Powers* **Anthony Burgess** £4.95

'Crowded, crammed, bursting with manic erudition, garlicky puns,
omnilingual jokes . . . (a novel) which meshes the real and personal-
ized history of the twentieth century' – Martin Amis

☐ *Life & Times of Michael K* **J. M. Coetzee** £2.95

The Booker Prize-winning novel: 'It is hard to convey . . . just what
Coetzee's special quality is. His writing gives off whiffs of Conrad, of
Nabokov, of Golding, of the Paul Theroux of *The Mosquito Coast*.
But he is none of these, he is a harsh, compelling new voice' –
Victoria Glendinning

☐ *The Stories of William Trevor* £5.95

'Trevor packs into each separate five or six thousand words more
richness, more laughter, more ache, more multifarious human-ness
than many good writers manage to get into a whole novel' – *Punch*

☐ *The Book of Laughter and Forgetting*
   Milan Kundera £3.95

'A whirling dance of a book . . . a masterpiece full of angels, terror,
ostriches and love . . . No question about it. The most important
novel published in Britain this year' – Salman Rushdie

KING PENGUIN

☐ *Selected Poems* **Tony Harrison** £3.95

Poetry Book Society Recommendation. 'One of the few modern poets who actually has the gift of composing poetry' – James Fenton in the *Sunday Times*

☐ *The Book of Laughter and Forgetting*
Milan Kundera £3.95

'A whirling dance of a book . . . a masterpiece full of angels, terror, ostriches and love . . . No question about it. The most important novel published in Britain this year' – Salman Rushdie in the *Sunday Times*

☐ *The Sea of Fertility* **Yukio Mishima** £9.95

Containing *Spring Snow, Runaway Horses, The Temple of Dawn* and *The Decay of the Angel*: 'These four remarkable novels are the most complete vision we have of Japan in the twentieth century' – Paul Theroux

☐ *The Hawthorne Goddess* **Glyn Hughes** £2.95

Set in eighteenth century Yorkshire where 'the heroine, Anne Wylde, represents the doom of nature and the land . . . Hughes has an arresting style, both rich and abrupt' – *The Times*

☐ *A Confederacy of Dunces* **John Kennedy Toole** £3.95

In this Pulitzer Prize-winning novel, in the bulky figure of Ignatius J. Reilly an immortal comic character is born. 'I succumbed, stunned and seduced . . . it is a masterwork of comedy' – *The New York Times*

☐ *The Last of the Just* **André Schwartz-Bart** £3.95

The story of Ernie Levy, the last of the just, who was killed at Auschwitz in 1943: 'An outstanding achievement, of an altogether different order from even the best of earlier novels which have attempted this theme' – John Gross in the *Sunday Telegraph*

KING PENGUIN

☐ *The White Hotel* **D. M. Thomas**   £3.95

'A major artist has once more appeared', declared the *Spectator* on the publication of this acclaimed, now famous novel which recreates the imagined case history of one of Freud's woman patients.

☐ *Dangerous Play: Poems 1974–1984*
Andrew Motion   £2.95

Winner of the John Llewelyn Rhys Memorial Prize. Poems and an autobiographical prose piece, *Skating*, by the poet acclaimed in the *TLS* as 'a natural heir to the tradition of Edward Thomas and Ivor Gurney'.

☐ *A Time to Dance* **Bernard MacLaverty**   £2.50

Ten stories, including 'My Dear Palestrina' and 'Phonefun Limited', by the author of *Cal*: 'A writer who has a real affinity with the short story form' – *The Times Literary Supplement*

☐ *Keepers of the House* **Lisa St Aubin de Terán**   £2.95

Seventeen-year-old Lydia Sinclair marries Don Diego Beltrán and goes to live on his family's vast, decaying Andean farm. This exotic and flamboyant first novel won the Somerset Maugham Award.

☐ *The Deptford Trilogy* **Robertson Davies**   £5.95

'Who killed Boy Staunton?' – around this central mystery is woven an exhilarating and cunningly contrived trilogy of novels: *Fifth Business, The Manticore* and *World of Wonders*.

☐ *The Stories of William Trevor*   £5.95

'Trevor packs into each separate five or six thousand words more richness, more laughter, more ache, more multifarious human-ness than many good writers manage to get into a whole novel' – *Punch*. 'Classics of the genre' – Auberon Waugh

A CHOICE OF PENGUINS

☐ *Further Chronicles of Fairacre* **'Miss Read'** £3.95

Full of humour, warmth and charm, these four novels – *Miss Clare Remembers, Over the Gate, The Fairacre Festival* and *Emily Davis* – make up an unforgettable picture of English village life.

☐ *Callanish* **William Horwood** £1.95

From the acclaimed author of *Duncton Wood*, this is the haunting story of Creggan, the captured golden eagle, and his struggle to be free.

☐ *Act of Darkness* **Francis King** £2.50

Anglo-India in the 1930s, where a peculiarly vicious murder triggers 'A terrific mystery story . . . a darkly luminous parable about innocence and evil' – *The New York Times*. 'Brilliantly successful' – *Daily Mail*. 'Unputdownable' – *Standard*

☐ *Death in Cyprus* **M. M. Kaye** £1.95

Holidaying on Aphrodite's beautiful island, Amanda finds herself caught up in a murder mystery in which no one, not even the attractive painter Steven Howard, is quite what they seem . . .

☐ *Lace* **Shirley Conran** £2.95

Lace is, quite simply, a publishing sensation: the story of Judy, Kate, Pagan and Maxine; the bestselling novel that teaches men about women, and women about themselves. 'Riches, bitches, sex and jetsetters' locations – they're all there' – *Sunday Express*

A CHOICE OF PENGUINS

☐ **West of Sunset** **Dirk Bogarde**   £1.95

'His virtues as a writer are precisely those which make him the most compelling screen actor of his generation,' is what *The Times* said about Bogarde's savage, funny, romantic novel set in the gaudy wastes of Los Angeles.

☐ **The Riverside Villas Murder** **Kingsley Amis**   £1.95

Marital duplicity, sexual discovery and murder with a thirties back-cloth: 'Amis in top form' – *The Times*. 'Delectable from page to page . . . effortlessly witty' – C. P. Snow in the *Financial Times*

☐ **A Dark and Distant Shore** **Reay Tannahill**   £3.95

Vilia is the unforgettable heroine, Kinveil Castle is her destiny, in this full-blooded saga spanning a century of Victoriana, empire, hatreds and love affairs. 'A marvellous blend of *Gone with the Wind* and *The Thorn Birds*. You will enjoy every page' – *Daily Mirror*

☐ **Kingsley's Touch** **John Collee**   £1.95

'Gripping . . . I recommend this chilling and elegantly written medical thriller' – *Daily Express*. 'An absolutely outstanding storyteller' – *Daily Telegraph*

☐ **The Far Pavilions** **M. M. Kaye**   £4.95

Holding all the romance and high adventure of nineteenth-century India, M. M. Kaye's magnificent, now famous, novel has at its heart the passionate love of an Englishman for Juli, his Indian princess. 'Wildly exciting' – *Daily Telegraph*

ENGLISH AND AMERICAN
LITERATURE IN PENGUINS

☐ *Emma* Jane Austen   £1.25

'I am going to take a heroine whom no one but myself will much like,' declared Jane Austen of Emma, her most spirited and controversial heroine in a comedy of self-deceit and self-discovery.

☐ *Tender is the Night* F. Scott Fitzgerald   £2.95

Fitzgerald worked on seventeen different versions of this novel, and its obsessions – idealism, beauty, dissipation, alcohol and insanity – were those that consumed his own marriage and his life.

☐ *The Life of Johnson* James Boswell   £2.95

Full of gusto, imagination, conversation and wit, Boswell's immortal portrait of Johnson is as near a novel as a true biography can be, and still regarded by many as the finest 'life' ever written. This shortened version is based on the 1799 edition.

☐ *A House and its Head* Ivy Compton-Burnett   £4.95

In a novel 'as trim and tidy as a hand-grenade' (as Pamela Hansford Johnson put it), Ivy Compton-Burnett penetrates the facade of a conventional, upper-class Victorian family to uncover a chasm of violent emotions – jealousy, pain, frustration and sexual passion.

☐ *The Trumpet Major* Thomas Hardy   £1.50

Although a vein of unhappy unrequited love runs through this novel, Hardy also draws on his warmest sense of humour to portray Wessex village life at the time of the Napoleonic wars.

☐ *The Complete Poems of Hugh MacDiarmid*

☐ Volume One   £8.95
☐ Volume Two   £8.95

The definitive edition of work by the greatest Scottish poet since Robert Burns, edited by his son Michael Grieve, and W. R. Aitken.

ENGLISH AND AMERICAN
LITERATURE IN PENGUINS

☐ *Main Street* **Sinclair Lewis**   £4.95

The novel that added an immortal chapter to the literature of America's Mid-West, *Main Street* contains the comic essence of Main Streets everywhere.

☐ *The Compleat Angler* **Izaak Walton**   £2.50

A celebration of the countryside, and the superiority of those in 1653, as now, who love *quietnesse, vertue* and, above all, *Angling*. 'No fish, however coarse, could wish for a doughtier champion than Izaak Walton' – Lord Home

☐ *The Portrait of a Lady* **Henry James**   £2.50

'One of the two most brilliant novels in the language', according to F. R. Leavis, James's masterpiece tells the story of a young American heiress, prey to fortune-hunters but not without a will of her own.

☐ *Hangover Square* **Patrick Hamilton**   £3.95

Part love story, part thriller, and set in the publands of London's Earls Court, this novel caught the conversational tone of a whole generation in the uneasy months before the Second World War.

☐ *The Rainbow* **D. H. Lawrence**   £2.50

Written between *Sons and Lovers* and *Women in Love*, *The Rainbow* covers three generations of Brangwens, a yeoman family living on the borders of Nottinghamshire.

☐ *Vindication of the Rights of Woman*
   Mary Wollstonecraft   £2.95

Although Walpole once called her 'a hyena in petticoats', Mary Wollstonecraft's vision was such that modern feminists continue to go back and debate the arguments so powerfully set down here.